# THIS
# IS
# MY
# TRUNK

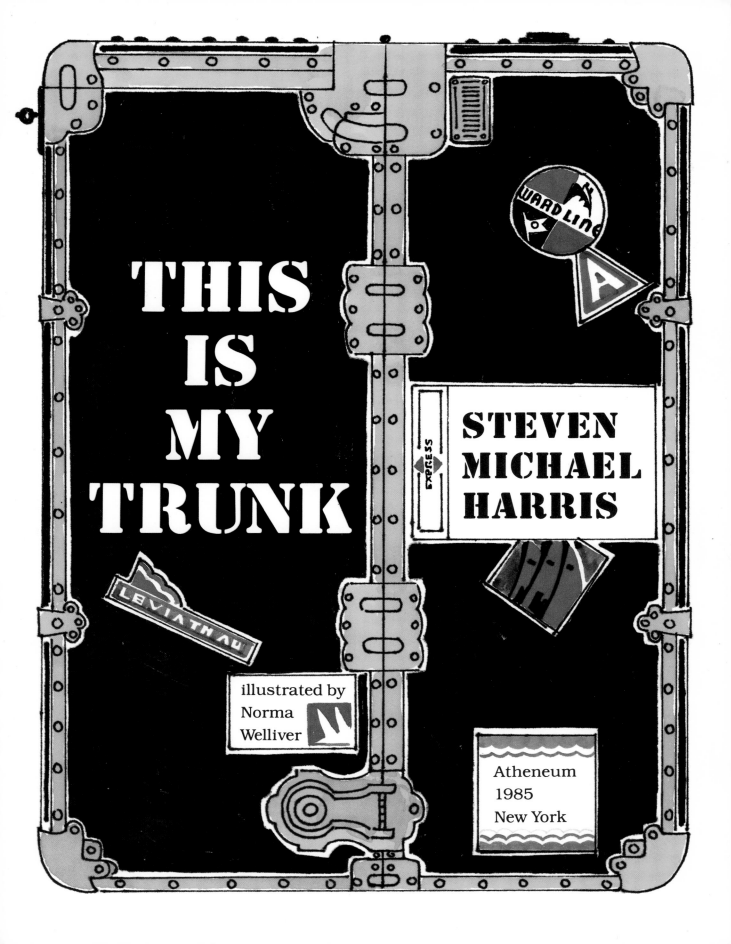

Library of Congress Cataloging in Publication Data

Harris, Steven Michael.
This is my trunk.

SUMMARY: An examination of a clown preparing for a
performance reveals the inside story of clown life
backstage at the circus.
1. Clowns—Juvenile literature.   2. Circus—Juvenile
literature.   [1. Clowns.   2. Circus]   I. Welliver, Norma,
ill.   II. Title.
GV1828.H37   1985     791.3'3'0924   [B]     85-7462
ISBN 0-689-31128-1

Published simultaneously in Canada by
Collier Macmillan Canada, Inc.
Text Set by Linoprint Composition, New York City
Printed and bound by South China Printing Company, Hong Kong
Typography by Mary Ahern
First Edition

# This is my trunk.

It is my closet,

my workshop,

my dresser,

and my office.

In it I keep my most important things.

I am a circus clown, and my trunk is where everything begins.

I work with many other clowns at the circus. Each one has his own trunk, and each trunk is different. When the circus arrives in town, the trunks are unloaded into an area called Clown Alley.

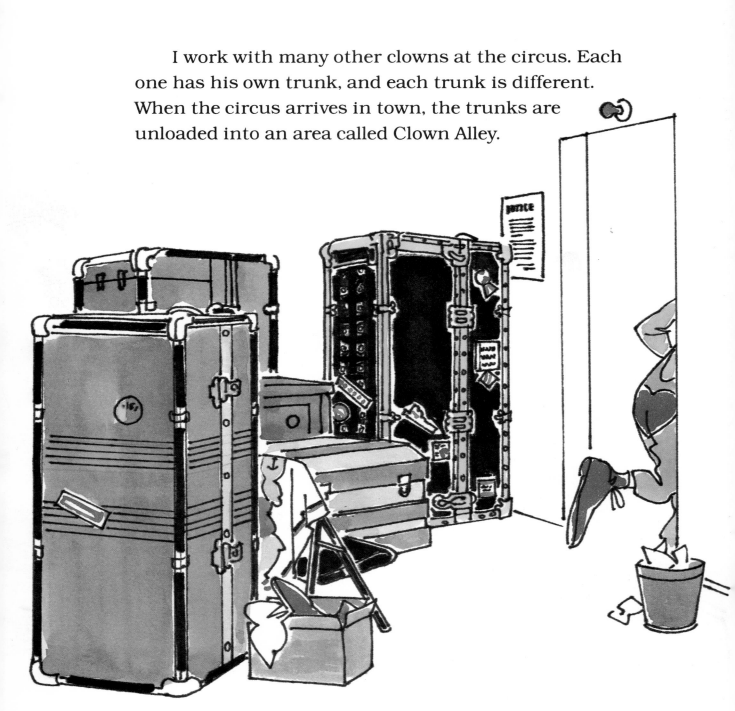

Clown Alley is as close as possible to the arena floor, so that clowns can be ready to entertain the audience if things go wrong.

One time, a door would not open for the elephant to enter the arena. The clowns kept the audience laughing until the door was fixed and the elephant could come out and do his act. The audience never knew anything had gone wrong.

Another time, the clowns rushed out and performed at one end of the arena under spotlight, while in the dark at the other end, workers rescued a trapeze artist. His tights had snagged and wrapped around the trapeze bar, leaving him tangled and exposed high above the arena floor. The clowns worked their funny routines, but this one time the trapeze act got more laughs.

When a safety net breaks, or when equipment doesn't go together easily between acts, or the truck carrying the cannon act stalls, or has trouble making it around a corner; the clowns are there until workmen can fix the problem.

Clowns must be ready to perform in case another performer gets hurt during one of the many dangerous acts. Luckily, this is very rare.

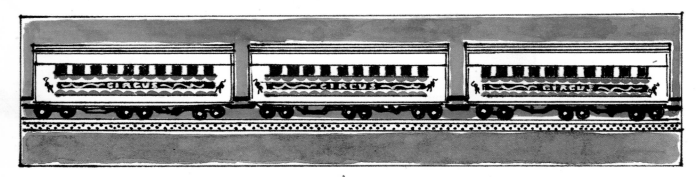

On the first day in a new town, I leave the circus train and come to the arena early to put my trunk in a good place. The first clown to arrive gets to pick the first spot. I like to be close to the door.

Then I open my trunk. It's heavy and strongly built. Everything I want is inside.

I keep a mirror,

paper, pens,

books,

a radio,

pictures of my girlfriends,

sunglasses,

a little fan,

needles and thread,

suntan lotion,

my lucky charm,

playing cards,

a backgammon board, shoe polish,

shoe and cloth dyes,

my coffee mug,

peanut butter,

a toothbrush—
anything that I might need—
in my trunk.

I grab a chair to sit in front of my trunk. Then I start to get ready for the show.

First, I undress and put my street clothes on a hanger. Then I put on my funny clown underwear over my regular underwear. It is part of my costume.

The white skull cap has holes in it for my ears, and it keeps my hair out of my face. It makes me look bald.

Now I am comfortable, and I don't have to worry about getting makeup on my good clothes or my costumes.

I use theatrical makeup that can be found at special stores such as magic and dancewear shops. Clown makeup is not as expensive as regular makeup, and it stays on a long time.

The white goes on first. This is the makeup I use the most, so I buy it in big one-pound cans. It is actually zinc oxide, the same thing lifeguards put on their noses to keep from getting sunburned. When I am in the sun for a long time wearing my makeup, I get sunburned under the other colors, but not under the white. Then I have red clown marks on my face without wearing any makeup at all.

I put a big glob of makeup in my hand, rub my palms together to spread the makeup evenly, then smear it over my face. When my face and neck are covered with white, I slap myself silly to make it look smooth. Using cotton swabs and a rag I scrape away some of the white. This is where I will apply other colors for the design of my face. Then I take a sock filled with talcum powder and dust a cloud of the white powder over the white makeup. This dries it and makes it stay on my face. I brush off the excess powder and now I look like a ghost.

The powder is bad to breathe, so I don't powder my face around the other clowns or near my own trunk.

Next, I put on the red, black and blue makeup… then powder again with the same white talc. I lightly brush off my face, and the makeup is finished.

It took me fifteen minutes, but I've had a lot of practice. My makeup will stay on all day. Sometimes circus people go swimming between shows on hot summer days. Even underwater, the makeup stays on perfectly.

The nose I wear is made from a painted ping-pong ball and clips to my nose. Other clowns wear rubber noses, putty noses, or put makeup on their own noses.

My wig is bald on top and has blue yak hair around the sides. Yak hair is stiff, which makes it look funnier, and it can be dyed many bright colors. It comes from a yak, a big, long-haired ox that lives in Tibet in Asia. You can see what a yak looks like when you go to the zoo, but you won't see any with blue hair!

bloo?

This is my best and favorite costume. It is very formal, with tails, vest, loose pants and white gloves.

My clown shoes are big and red. They were made especially to fit my own feet on the inside and be extra big on the outside. They feel just like ordinary shoes when I wear them.

Funny makeup, wig, costume, and shoes. I'm all done.

I wear this costume unless I need to be a cowboy for a western gag, or a nurse for a hospital gag, or any time I play a different person. A "gag" is a clown play or skit. Many gags might be going on at the same time around the arena floor. We'll play any characters that might be funny as a clown: a clown Playboy bunny, a clown president, or even a clown extraterrestrial.

Sometimes I wear special clothes for special tricks. I have a big loose coat that I dive into during one routine and pants that rip away when a rope is pulled, leaving me in my funny clown underwear.

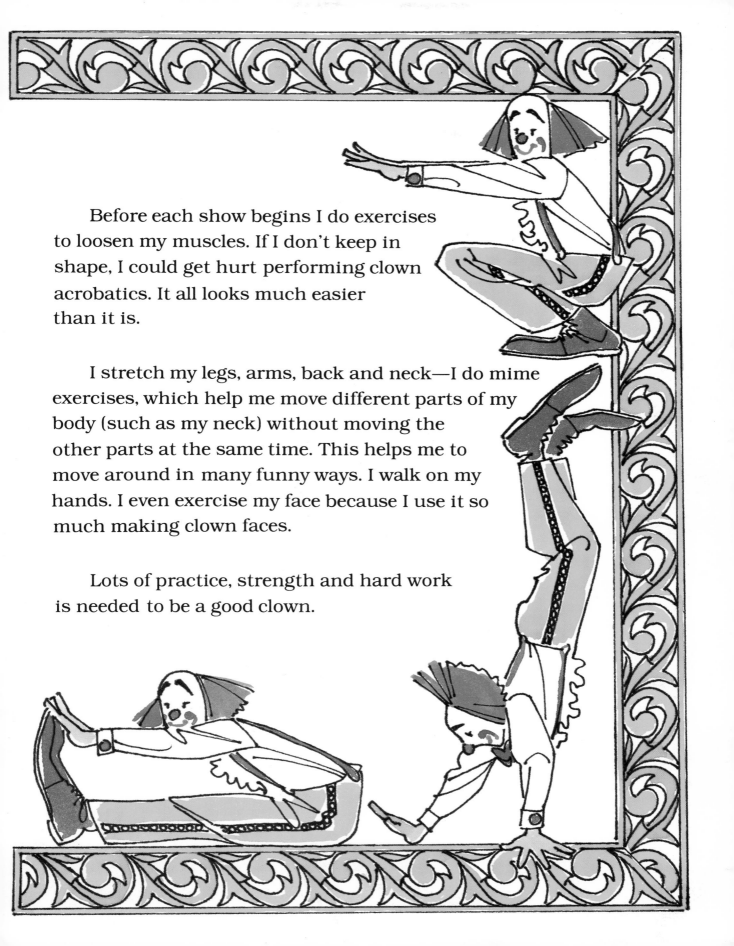

Before each show begins I do exercises to loosen my muscles. If I don't keep in shape, I could get hurt performing clown acrobatics. It all looks much easier than it is.

I stretch my legs, arms, back and neck—I do mime exercises, which help me move different parts of my body (such as my neck) without moving the other parts at the same time. This helps me to move around in many funny ways. I walk on my hands. I even exercise my face because I use it so much making clown faces.

Lots of practice, strength and hard work is needed to be a good clown.

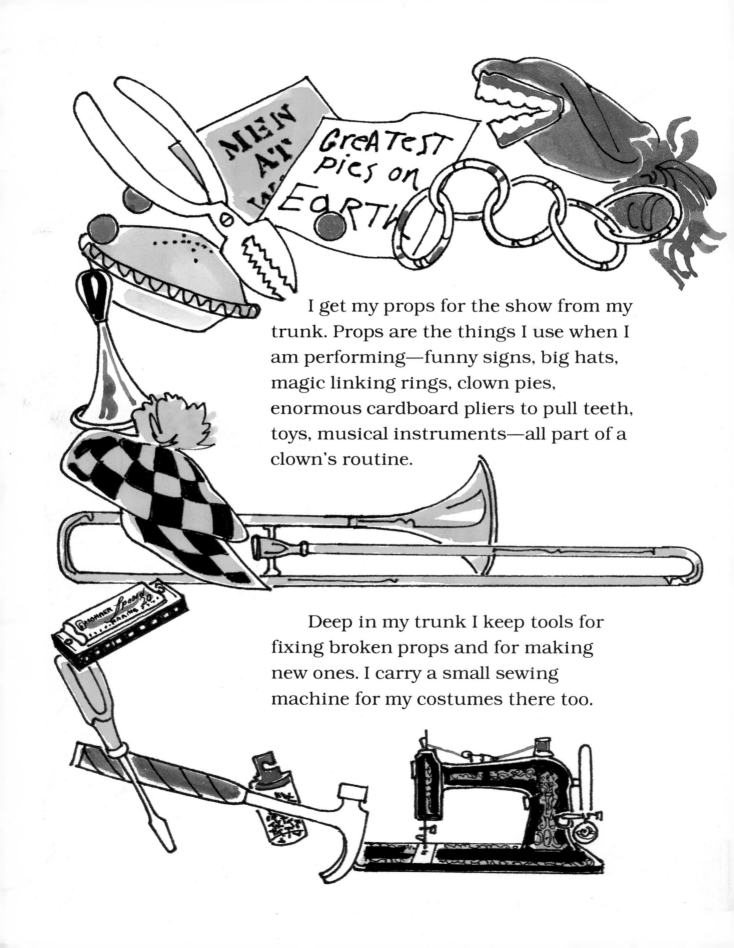

I get my props for the show from my trunk. Props are the things I use when I am performing—funny signs, big hats, magic linking rings, clown pies, enormous cardboard pliers to pull teeth, toys, musical instruments—all part of a clown's routine.

Deep in my trunk I keep tools for fixing broken props and for making new ones. I carry a small sewing machine for my costumes there too.

I am a "whiteface" clown.

John is an "Auguste" (ah-goost) clown. He uses special flesh-colored makeup some places where I use white. Auguste clowns—especially in Germany and other parts of Europe—act goofier than the other clowns. Though now, in America, the style of makeup doesn't always tell how a clown may act.

There are also "character" clowns like Clem…

and "tramp" clowns such as Will.

Each clown creates his own image. Clowns may act and look very much like great clowns of the past. They might copy little quirks, movements, parts of costumes and makeup…but a good clown tries to find a character that is all his own.

My clown character is very formal. He stands very straight. He walks fast with stiff and jerky movements, and when he looks around, his head slides from side to side in a funny way. My character gets excited doing his own tricks and claps for himself a lot.

While I am backstage in Clown Alley getting everything ready for the show, the audience starts finding their seats in the arena. Some clowns perform before the actual show as the people arrive in what is called the "come-in." Clowns might be anywhere during this time. Some might be hidden right in the seats. You should always look out for clowns before the show.

Soon, when all the spectators have arrived, it's time for the show to begin!

After the tiger act, we clowns do the baker's gag. I am the baker in a white apron and a big white chef's hat.

John plays the baker's assistant. His know-it-all clown character is mischievous, bold and always looking for trouble. But usually things go wrong for him in the end.

Clem is the husband of the couple that comes to buy pies in the baker's shop. Clem is very goofy, timid and stupid as a clown. (He is actually a smart, talented man.) He has a funny clown walk that makes his legs look like they are made of rubber. He is also acrobatic, so his character takes several outlandish falls, especially when his wife hits him with her oversized purse.

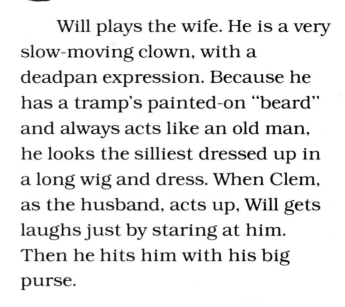

Will plays the wife. He is a very slow-moving clown, with a deadpan expression. Because he has a tramp's painted-on "beard" and always acts like an old man, he looks the silliest dressed up in a long wig and dress. When Clem, as the husband, acts up, Will gets laughs just by staring at him. Then he hits him with his big purse.

During the gag, I happily bake pies in my "clown oven," making the "Greatest Pies On Earth" (says our big sign). Behind my back, John puts old shoes, cement and dynamite into the pies. Clem tries to please his wife (Will) with a pie from our shop. First she bites into a shoe and knocks Clem down. Then she bites into the concrete pie and pulls from her mouth a huge set of clown teeth stuck to the pie. Of course, she hits her husband again with her purse. When Clem tries to bring her another pie, she takes a swing at him. He ducks and accidentally throws the pie under John's chair. The pie explodes, sending John into the oven. I put another pie into the oven with John and close the door, never knowing anything went wrong—and the gag is over.

In the other acts I can play

a cop…

or a doctor…

or be a one-man band.

I can juggle rings, clubs,
balls…fire ("ouch")…almost
anything.

Between acts we clowns relax.

When the show is over I put away my costumes and take off my makeup. I use vegetable oil to soften and remove it because soap and water won't do the job.

Then I take a shower and dress in my street clothes.

If the circus is moving on after the show, I pack my props and costumes very carefully so they will arrive safely at the next town. Then I close the trunk.

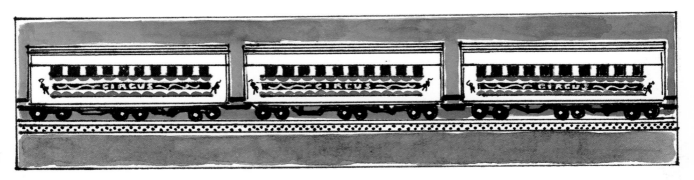

When I'm ready to go home to the circus train, where I live, nobody, except you, will be able to tell what I do.

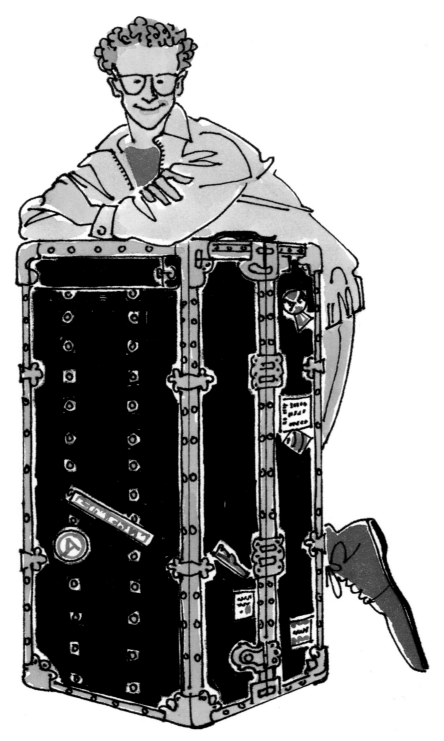

I am a circus clown…
but all of my secrets are locked in

# MY TRUNK.